As Luck Would Have It

• FROM THE BROTHERS GRIMM •

Robert D. San Souci
Illustrated by Daniel San Souci

August House LittleFolk
ATLANTA

To Skyla Anders Leventon—RSS
For Carl, Holly and Baby Jun—DSS

Published 2008 by August House LittleFolk • 3500 Piedmont Road NE, Suite 310, Atlanta, Georgia 30305
404-442-4420 • www.augusthouse.com

The illustrations were painted with Windsor Newton watercolors on DeArches 300 lb. hot press paper.
Prismacolor pencils were used for highlights. The text is set in Jimbo Condensed. Book design by Joy Freeman.
Manufactured in Korea   10 9 8 7 6 5 4 3 2 1

LIBRARY OF CONGRESS CATALOGING-IN-PUBLICATION DATA
San Souci, Robert D.
As luck would have it : from the Brothers Grimm / Robert D. San Souci ; illustrated by Daniel San Souci.
p. cm.
Summary: Left to take care of the family farm and fortune while their parents are away, twin bear cubs
Juniper and Jonas have a series of mishaps before outwitting three thieves, in spite of themselves.
ISBN 978-0-87483-833-6 (alk. paper)
[1. Folklore--Germany.] I. San Souci, Daniel, ill. II. Grimm, Jacob, 1785-1863. III. Grimm, Wilhelm, 1786-1859. IV. Title.
PZ8.1.S227Asd 2008
398.2—dc22
[E]
2008000965

AUGUST HOUSE   PUBLISHERS   ATLANTA

There once were twins named Jonas and Juniper.
They lived with their mother and father at the edge of a forest.

One day their parents called them in from their chores. "Grandmother is very sick," said their mother. "Your father and I must go care for her."

"Take care of the house and fields," their father added. "Keep a watch on the door at all times. I have heard the woods are full of thieves."

Papa led the twins down to the cellar and showed them a loose brick in the corner. "Under this is a sack of gold coins. It is the family fortune. You must both promise never to touch the brick or open the sack."

"We will never let the door out of sight," Jonas promised.

Juniper added, "Neither of us will touch the brick or open the sack."

Satisfied, their parents set out for Grandmother's house.

The next day, Jonas went to plow the fields. But after driving the ox team back and forth several times, he thought to himself, "There is no need for me to keep steering the oxen. They can do the work very well themselves."

Jonas told the creatures to keep doing what they were doing while he rested. But when he woke up, the oxen had wandered to and fro.

"What a mess!" he scolded. "After lunch, you will have to plow the field all over again!"

Jonas was so eager for his midday meal, he left without tying the oxen.

All the while, Juniper was fixing lunch. She began heating a sausage over the chimney fire.

As the meat sizzled, she decided, "The sausage is quite able to fry itself. I am wasting time when I could be drawing cider to go with our lunch."

She took a mug and went down to the cellar, where she opened the cider tap. But as the cider ran into the mug, she thought, "Oh, dear! The door is open, and the dog isn't tied. He might snatch the sausage out of the pan."

Leaving the mug to finish filling itself, she ran upstairs.

As luck would have it, the dog, sausage in mouth,
was running out the door.
Juniper gave chase, but the
pup was too fast for her.

"What's done is done," sighed Juniper. Suddenly she broke into a run. She hadn't turned the cider tap off!

From the top of the steps, she saw the cider had poured itself all over the cellar floor.

"Dear me!" she cried. "I must tidy up."

Juniper took two flour sacks from the kitchen and toted them downstairs. She began strewing the flour around to cover the cider. When she had finished, she said, "How neat and clean everything looks—like the fields after first snowfall."

Just then, Jonas came home. "What's for lunch?" he asked.

"Bread and milk," replied Juniper.

"I had hoped for sausage and cider," her brother said.

"So had I," agreed Juniper. "But while I was frying the sausage, I went down to draw your cider, and the dog ran off with the sausage. While I

was running after the dog, the cider ran out on the floor, so I had to use flour to tidy up."

"Oh, Juniper!" Jonas said. "You should have thought about the dog before you began cooking! You should have turned off the cider tap before you left the cellar! And you should have mopped up the cider."

"How smart you are, Jonas!" Juniper exclaimed. "I will remember next time."

As luck would have it, when Jonas went back to the field, he found that the oxen had tried to drink from the pond and tumbled in. Jonas ran to rescue them, but as he pulled them out, they broke the pond wall. Water gushed out and turned the freshly plowed field into a sea of mud.

"You foolish animals!" wailed Jonas. He began to fling gobs of mud at the oxen. Startled, the beasts ran off, while the plow bounced behind them, breaking into pieces. Jonas, chasing them and shouting, frightened them more, so they ran all the faster until he lost sight of them.

Meanwhile, Juniper set off to market to sell their goat cheese. When she reached the top of the hill that led to town, she stopped to rest.

But when she set down her sack, as luck would have it, one of the cheeses tumbled out and rolled down the hill toward town.

"That cheese is eager to get to market!" Juniper exclaimed. "Perhaps they all want to go ahead."

Sure enough! Each cheese rolled down the hill just like the first when Juniper spun them on their way. While the cheeses were making their way to market, Juniper took a short nap.

But when she reached town, no one admitted having seen her cheeses.

"Those foolish cheeses have gotten themselves lost," she decided.

When Juniper returned home, she found Jonas weary and covered with mud. When he told her what had happened, she said, "The oxen are as foolish as the cheeses that ran away." Then she told Jonas her story, and the two of them agreed that neither oxen nor cheeses could be trusted.

As luck would have it, the following day three peddlers came by, selling pots and pans. They assured Juniper their wares were the best, so when they offered her the lot for a small price, Juniper agreed.

How happy her mother would be with so many pots and pans! But she sighed. "Oh, dear. I have no money to buy things with." Suddenly she said, "Papa left money in the cellar under the loose brick in the corner. I promised not to touch it, but if you would go and fetch payment, I'm sure it would be all right."

Eagerly the peddlers (who were really thieves who had stolen the pots and pans) unpacked their wares, ran down the stairs, found the sack of gold, and hurried away without so much as a "good day" to Juniper.

"They must have important business to be off in such a rush," thought Juniper.

When Jonas returned home, he found his sister putting the pots on the kitchen shelves. When she told him about the good price she got from the peddlers, he ran down to the cellar. In a minute he was back, groaning, "Oh, Juniper! You let thieves run off with our fortune!"

"I let the cider make a mess of the cellar and let Mama's cheeses run away," wailed Juniper. "And now I've lost the family gold."

"I let the oxen run off and turn the field into a sea of mud," Jonas said. "Mama and Papa will be very angry."

"What are we going to do?" asked Juniper.

"I'll go after the thieves!" Jonas decided. "If I get our gold back, Papa and Mama won't be so angry."

"I'm coming too!" cried Juniper as her brother ran out the door.

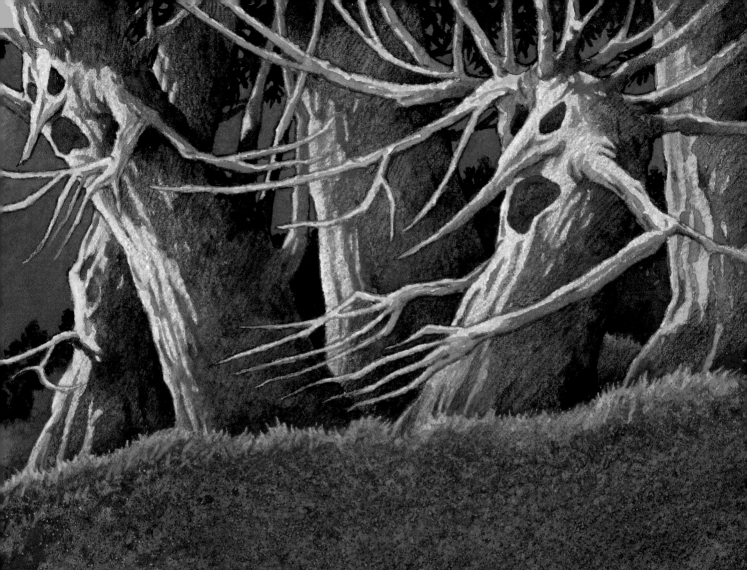

Then she said to herself, "I'd better bring something to eat and drink, since the chase may be a long one." So she wrapped some biscuits in a napkin and filled a jar with milk.

As she was leaving, she remembered Papa had told them to keep watch on the door. So she took it off its hinges and tied it on her back. But as she went along, she decided, "This door is heavy enough by itself. I can't carry the milk jar and biscuits, too. I will hang them on the door, and let it share my burden."

Then she kept on after Jonas, happy to have lightened her load.

Soon Juniper caught up with her brother at the forest's edge. When Jonas saw the door, he praised her for remembering their father's instructions to guard it. The two searched for the thieves until dark. At last, afraid of wild beasts, they climbed a tree to spend the night.

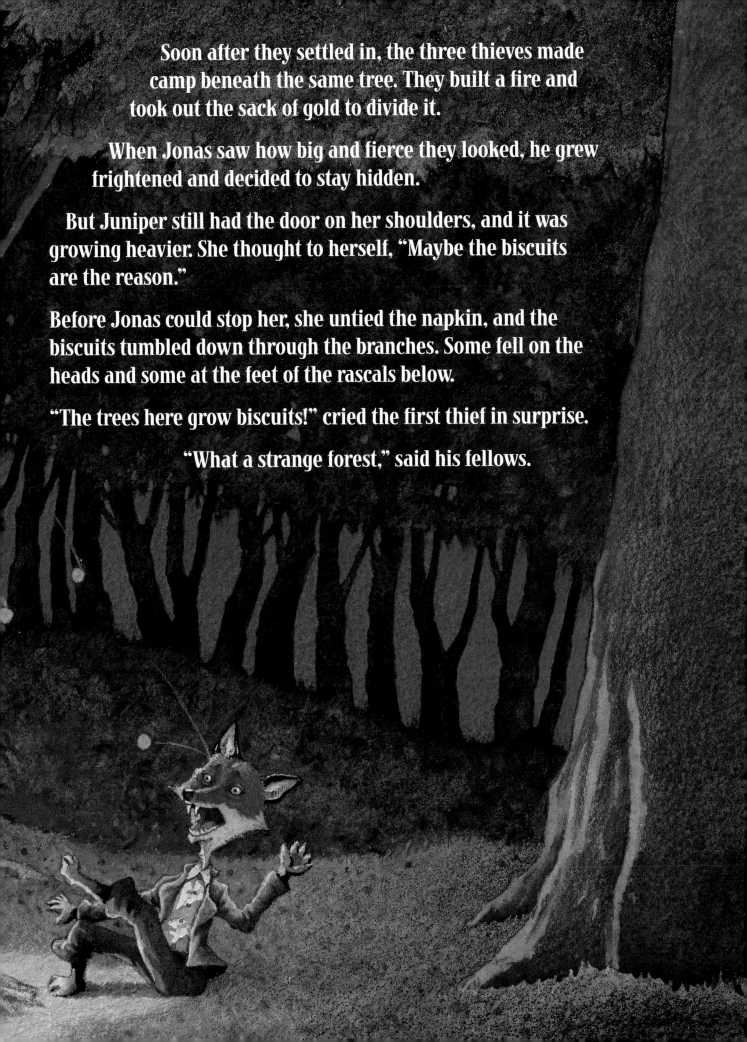

Soon after they settled in, the three thieves made camp beneath the same tree. They built a fire and took out the sack of gold to divide it.

When Jonas saw how big and fierce they looked, he grew frightened and decided to stay hidden.

But Juniper still had the door on her shoulders, and it was growing heavier. She thought to herself, "Maybe the biscuits are the reason."

Before Jonas could stop her, she untied the napkin, and the biscuits tumbled down through the branches. Some fell on the heads and some at the feet of the rascals below.

"The trees here grow biscuits!" cried the first thief in surprise.

"What a strange forest," said his fellows.

A little later, Juniper found the weight of the door still bothered her. "It must be the milk jar that's so heavy," she whispered to Jonas. "I'm going to pour it out."

Before he could stop her, she emptied the pitcher. Milk spattered down over the thieves.

"Now it's raining milk!" said the second thief, uneasily.

"This forest is growing stranger," said the first thief.

"Perhaps it is enchanted," suggested the third. "Or cursed."

They began to look around fearfully for other wonders or terrors the woods might serve up.

High above, Juniper was wondering, "Could it be the door that's such a burden on me?"

Quietly, so as not to awaken her dozing brother, Juniper untied the door. As luck would have it, her skirts got caught on the hinges. Hastily, she shook Jonas awake and whispered, "I'm letting the door go. But since it doesn't seem to want to fall alone, I'm going with it."

Startled, Jonas made a grab for her.

Too late! Juniper crashed down, riding the door through snapping, flapping branches, giving a shriek that was half excitement and half fear.

Hearing the racket, the thieves, who had been asleep by the fire, rose up. "A monster! A demon! A dragon!" they shouted.

Then the door fell on top of them, knocking them senseless, while they neatly cushioned Juniper's fall.

Jonas scrambled down, untangled Juniper, and grabbed the gold, while Juniper took the door. They were away long before the thieves came to their senses.

When they got home,
Jonas said, "Well, Juniper, you saved our fortune."

"The door was the real hero," his sister protested.
"I just followed where it led."

They replaced the gold and the door.

The next day they worked together to clean the cellar and repair the pond and plow. Together they searched for, and found, the missing oxen. They took turns plowing the field properly. Somehow, when they put their heads together, things didn't turn out silly or badly. So, as luck would have it, all was fine when their parents returned, and the farm continued to prosper.